Tundra Books, an imprint of Penguin Random House Canada Young Readers,
a Penguin Random House Company

Library and Archives Canada Cataloguing in Publication
Fleck, Jay, author, illustrator
Tilly and Tank / written and illustrated by Jay Fleck.
Issued in print and electronic formats.
ISBN 978-1-101-91786-2 (bound). — ISBN 978-1-101-91788-6 (epub)
I. Title.
PZ7.1.F54Ti 2018   j813'.6   C2015-905753-1
C2015-905754-X

TO TARA AND KIRSTEN

Published simultaneously in the United States of America by Tundra Books of
Northern New York, an imprint of Penguin Random House Canada Young Readers,
a Penguin Random House Company

Library of Congress Control Number: 2015955123

Edited by Tara Walker
Designed by Terri Nimmo
The artwork in this book was rendered
in pencil and colored digitally.
The text was set in Neutraface.
Printed and bound in China

www.penguinrandomhouse.ca

2   3   4   5   22   21   20   19   18

Penguin
Random House
tundra   TUNDRA BOOKS

Tilly & Tank

JAY FLECK

tundra

Tilly was taking her morning stroll
when she noticed something strange
in the distance.

It had a trunk and a tail, just like she did.
But it was a very curious shade of green.
Must be a different kind of elephant,
thought Tilly.

Tank was on his morning patrol when he
detected something strange ahead.

It had a barrel and a turret,
just like he did.

But it was a very curious
shade of blue.

Must be an enemy tank, thought Tank. His alarm sounded:
WEE-OOO! WEE-OOO! WEE-OOO!

Tilly walked right up to the noisy green elephant.
She took a close look at his trunk . . .

his tail . . .

his eyes . . .

and behind his ears.

Then she cleared her throat and said:

Hello.

Tank responded with a . . .

BOOOOO

Tilly was so startled . . .

she shut her eyes tight and ran.

Tank was puzzled.

Where did the enemy go?

Tilly peeked out from her hiding spot.

Was that BOOM just a very, very loud hello?
Tilly wondered.

She decided to try again.

Slowly and carefully,
Tilly tiptoed closer . . .

and closer . . .

until she was just close enough to . . .

BOOP

. . . give the green elephant a friendly tap.

Tank's alarm sounded again:
WEE-OOO! WEE-OOO! WEE-OOO!

Tilly shut her eyes tight and ran.

Tank was even more puzzled.
Why doesn't the enemy stay and fight? he thought.

Tilly ran so fast she tripped over a rock
and landed with a thump . . .

in a bed of flowers.

Flowers? This gave Tilly an idea.

Tank saw the enemy returning with a strange object.

Is that a weapon? he wondered.
Tank stood strong and responded with a . . .

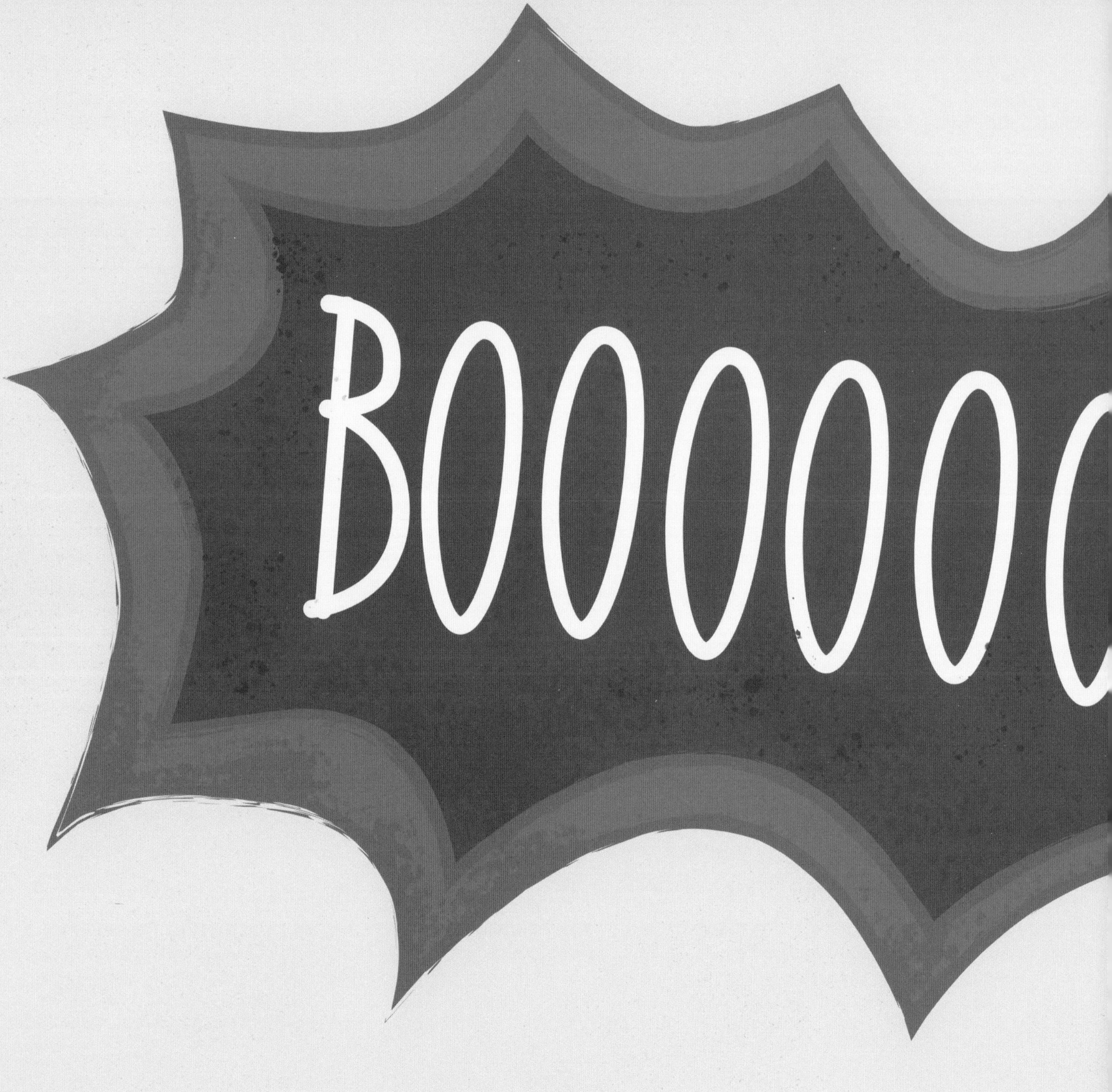
BOOOOO

And off ran Tilly again.

But this time Tank observed that
the enemy had left something behind.

Its weapon!

He scanned the object and discovered . . .

. . . a flower?

Oh no! thought Tank.

He had been wrong. That wasn't an enemy.

That was a friend!

Tilly was nervous when
she saw the green elephant approaching.

Then she saw what he was carrying . . .

. . . a magnificent bouquet!

Tank dropped the flowers at Tilly's feet.

Tilly smiled as she sat next to her new green friend.
Tank's alarm was replaced by a happy sound
from deep inside his engine:
THUMP-THUMP, THUMP-THUMP, THUMP-THUMP.

There was a happy sound coming
from deep inside Tilly too:
THUMP-THUMP, THUMP-THUMP, THUMP-THUMP.